"HELLO READING books are a perfect introduction to reading. Brief sentences full of word repetition and full-color pictures stress visual clues to help a child take the first important steps toward reading. Mastering these storybooks will build children's reading confidence and give them the enthusiasm to stand on their own in the world of words."

—Bee Cullinan
Past President of the International Reading
Association, Professor in New York University's
Early Childhood and Elementary Education Program

"Readers aren't born, they're made. Desire is planted—planted by parents who work at it."

—Jim Trelease
author of *The Read-Aloud Handbook*

"When I was a classroom reading teacher, I recognized the importance of good stories in making children understand that reading is more than just recognizing words. I saw that children who have ready access to storybooks get excited about reading. They also make noticeably greater gains in reading comprehension. The development of the HELLO READING stories grows out of this experience."

—Harriet Ziefert
M.A.T., New York University School of Education
Author, Language Arts Module,
Scholastic Early Childhood Program

For Allison

VIKING
Published by the Penguin Group
Viking Penguin, a division of Penguin Books USA Inc.,
375 Hudson Street, New York, New York 10014, U.S.A.
Penguin Books Ltd, 27 Wrights Lane, London W8 5TZ, England
Penguin Books Australia Ltd, Ringwood, Victoria, Australia
Penguin Books Canada Ltd, 2801 John Street, Markham, Ontario, Canada L3R 1B4
Penguin Books (N.Z.) Ltd, 182-190 Wairau Road, Auckland 10, New Zealand

Penguin Books Ltd, Registered Offices: Harmondsworth, Middlesex, England

First published in 1991 by Viking Penguin, a division of Penguin Books USA Inc.

1 3 5 7 9 10 8 6 4 2

Text copyright © Harriet Ziefert, 1991
Illustrations copyright © David Prebenna, 1991
All rights reserved
Library of Congress catalog card number: 90-50713
ISBN 0-670-83858-6

Printed in Singapore for Harriet Ziefert, Inc.

A Car Trip for Mole and Mouse

Harriet Ziefert
Pictures by David Prebenna

VIKING

"This is a nice day," said Mole.
"Let's take a car trip."

"Okay," said Mouse.
"Let's take a trip.
 Let's go to a flea market."

Mole got the car.
Mouse got the map.

"You drive the car," said Mouse.
"I will read the map.

And everything will be just fine."

Mole drove.

Mouse read the map.
And everything was just fine!

"I see a traffic circle,"
said Mole.
"What do I do?"

"Wait," said Mouse.
"I am looking at the map."

"Hurry!" said Mole.
"I don't know where to go."

Mole drove around and
around and around
the traffic circle.

At last Mouse said, "Take the road over the bridge."

"I don't like bridges," said Mole.

"Then take the tunnel
under the bridge,"
said Mouse.

"Good," said Mole.
"I like tunnels."

"It is dark in here,"
said Mouse.
"I can't read the map."

"That's okay," said Mole.
"I know all about tunnels."

Soon Mole and Mouse
were out of the tunnel.

"I'm hungry!" said Mole.

"I'll look for a place to stop," said Mouse.

Mole and Mouse stopped
at a stand.

Mole got ice cream.
Mouse got popcorn.

And everything was just fine!

"Get off here for the flea market," said Mouse.

Mole got off at the exit.
He went down the road and…

everything was not just fine!

"Don't worry!" said Mouse.
"I'll look at the map.
    We can go another way."

"No," said Mole.
"You take too long.
I'm going this way!"

"All right. All right," said Mouse.
"We can go your way."

"We're here," said Mole.
"We're here!"

"I got us here," said Mouse.

Mole bought a desk.

And Mouse bought a chair.

And everything was just fine!